Table of Con

CW01240003

HARD Wright

A Straight To Gay Romance Law Enforcement Story

(First Time for Everything Series)

By B.T. Haiyes

Chapter 1
JOSH

"You ready to give up?" I stared down my opponent with a satisfied smirk.

My arm was bulging, the strength of my forearm pushed to the limit, as I held my opponents hand in place.

All around us the patrons in the bar let loose yells of encouragement — with my friends behind me loudest of them all.

I breathed slowly, keeping my cool even as the tabletop bit into my elbow, but I was determined to win this arm wrestling match.

My friends and co-workers from the police station were all cheering me on. I even heard someone behind me yell that I had to win this, or they'd never let me live it down.

I chuckled. I was confident I was going to win. So, I comfortably stared down the bulging-eyed red-faced man opposite, and held his hand firmly in place.

He, on the other hand, tried to put everything he had behind his.

When this guy tossed an open challenge of an arm wrestle our way — after he'd made a stupid remark about all police cops being unfit — I was the only one in my group who took him up on it.

This total stranger had wandered right up to me and my friends. We were all gathered in our favorite bar, raising one last glass in cheers to celebrate the fact that one of our own was retiring today.

Arthur, (my former training officer and a good friend of mine), was finally hanging up his hat. He'd lasted longer than most, calling it quits at the age of sixty.

So, when this kid — who looked barely a day over 21 — had come up to us with a chip on his shoulder, I figured I'd take him down a peg.

No way was I going to let some punk ruin my friends retirement party.

The kid — *Tate, I think his name was?* — had done a double take when he took in my well built six foot four inch frame.

Tate was no slouch either, I'd give him that. He had the frame — along with the douche-level sleeveless teeshirt to match — of a bodybuilder.

But, one thing about all of those muscles on him, was that while they may be pretty, they weren't as functional as the real strength I'd built up over the years.

Tate's face was now beet-red, and I laughed when he refused to give up. I had to hand it to him, he was tenacious.

I felt Arthur place a hand on my shoulder, and I glanced up. "Come on, Josh. Stop playing around with the kid," Arthur said with an amused look on his face. Waving a dismissive hand at my red-faced opponent, Arthur continued. "Just take the damn win."

I nodded. Turning my attention back towards Tate, I flexed my forearm, and in one fell swoop, slapped his hand down on the table.

The entire bar erupted into cheers and applause, and I was immediately swamped with pats on the back and 'atta boys' from my friends.

"You tried your best, kid," I said honestly, as the kid rose from his seat with a surly grumble. "But I was better. Not bad for a *pudgy* cop, I reckon."

Tate grunted noncommittally, and moved to rejoin his group of snickering friends. But, before he made it half a step, I spoke up. "I think you're forgetting something?"

The kid looked at me confused, until he saw me rubbing my fingers and thumb together in that universal 'money' motion. "Fifty bucks to the winner. That was our bet."

He let loose a low swear, and snatched his wallet from his back pocket.

Pulling a crisp fifty from it, the kid slapped it on the table, and then quickly hustled off through the jostling crowd to go lick his wounds with his friends.

Plucking the fifty off the table, I lifted it triumphantly into the air. "Daisy!" I yelled out, addressing the bartender.

Everyone at the station came here so often that we were on a first name basis with Daisy.

"The next round of drinks..." I clapped Arthur on the shoulder, as he raised his beer glass to me in congratulations, "...are On ME!" I shouted.

The bar erupted with noise once again, and over the sounds of celebration, Daisy shouted back. "I don't think that's gonna cover it," she said with a laugh, indicating the fifty in my hand. "But I'll put it on your tab."

I returned her smile, giving her a grateful wink, before turning to speak to Arthur. "And what will you be having, old man?" I gave his beer glass a short nod, "another beer, or maybe something a bit stronger?"

Arthur shook his head ruefully. "Enough with the *old man*. I can still plenty put you on your ass," he said with a chuckle. "Just another beer for me. My wife, Sandra, made me quit hard liquor. Hell, even my son has me trying out some of his craft beers." Arthur mirrored my look of disgust at the thought of those artisan drinks.

"Why would your son do that to you?" I said in mock horror, giving Arthur a comical look of concern, as I placed a hand on his shoulder. "Do you need another drink to wash away the memory?"

Arthur brushed off my hand with a chortle. "My boy's a good kid. But his taste in beer? He gets that from his mother."

"Well, that's why you'll never see me settling down," I said with a laugh.

Arthur paused for a moment at that, giving me a quickly sobering look.

'Ah shit,' I thought to myself. *'I recognize that look...'*

"Before you say it..." I began, but Arthur waved me off.

"I know you don't want to hear it Josh, but I gotta say it again. Look at this," Arthur waved a hand up at the banner that stretched out over the bar.

The banner read, *Happy Retirement — 25 Years Of Service.*

"Twenty five years. That's a hell of a long time on the force," Arthur continued, giving me a meaningful glance. "I've seen a lot over the years. A lot of bad stuff. But I stayed, and kept going for so long because I had something besides the job to live for."

It was an old argument that the two of us had over the years.

I joined the force at the age of 24. And Arthur — my former training officer — had taken me under his wing.

I'll be the first to admit that being a detective is pretty much my whole life. I've never wanted to do or be anything else.

Which also meant I had no time for dating. And at the age of 32, I still didn't feel ready yet to settle down with anyone. And I certainly didn't want the distraction of being in a committed relationship.

And, as a gay man, I wasn't attracting the kind of guy I wanted to settle down with. There are plenty of gay badge bunnies out there, but they were always more turned on by the idea of my job, than by me.

Don't get me wrong, one time hookups came a plenty — and I loved it. I'd simply hop onto a dating app, find a guy, and then get that release by the end of the night.

And then the next day I was right back at work. It worked for me — uncomplicated with no strings attached — and that's how I liked it.

"I hear ya, Arthur, I do." I draped a friendly arm around my friends shoulders. "But you don't have to worry about me. Tonight, all you need to worry about is getting another drink!"

As I began to lead Arthur over to the bar, one of our group suddenly yelled out. *"Arthur! Your son, Ben, is here!"*

And at that, both Arthur and I turned towards the entrance of the bar to find a blond-haired man entering the establishment.

"Ben!" Arthur called out to the man, hands raised, as he went over to greet him.

I watched on as the two men embraced for a long moment, before Arthur turned around to face the crowd. "My son Ben, everyone!" The crowd cheered in response.

It took a few more moments for the raucous celebration to come down a few notches, and I took that time to go and grab myself another beer.

While I watched Daisy pour my drink, I soon felt a tap on my shoulder.

Looking over, I saw Arthur standing side by side with Ben, with his arm draped around him.

And up close — now that I could see him much more clearly — Ben made me do a double take.

I hadn't gotten a good look at him from across the bar. But, getting up close to Ben now, this grown man looked nothing like he had done in Arthur's family photos.

In the photos — atop Arthur's desk back at the station — there had been a skinny college kid stood in between Arthur and his wife.

I'd never met Ben before. He was already a year into pre-med when I'd met Arthur, back when I was a rookie.

Still, I had heard plenty about the guy in passing. Arthur was incredibly proud of Ben.

So I did a poor job at hiding the look of surprise on my face, when Arthur introduced me to his pride and joy.

Ben stood only a few inches shorter than myself. Yet every inch of him seemed firm and surprisingly muscled for his slender yet well-built frame.

And Ben's tight white teeshirt and skinny jeans, didn't do much to hide his physique either. He still had that slender build from those pictures. However, now, taut sinewy muscle lined his biceps and forearms.

It seemed like Ben had filled out a lot over the last few years.

Between his dress sense, handsome features — and his crystal blue eyes — Ben looked next to nothing like Arthur. Except they both shared a very distinctive sharp square jaw.

"Josh? You alright?" Arthur asked, and I snapped my gaping mouth shut once I realized I'd been staring.

Arthur knew I was gay. In fact, the whole damn station knew I was gay. But, the last thing Arthur needed to know was that I found Ben attractive.

My good friend didn't have a problem with my sexuality, but he might have a problem with me personally if I made a move on Ben.

"Uh, yes, of course. I'm Josh," I quickly wiped my sweaty palm on my jeans, and held it out to Ben.

"Ben," the blond replied, as he clasped my hand firmly.

"Good to meet you," I continued, giving his hand a brief shake. Ben's grip was impressively firm. "Your dad's told me a lot about you."

"All of it good, I hope?" Ben said, his melodious voice captivating me.

"Mostly." I replied, chuckling at the shared affronted look on both Arthur's and Ben's faces. "He told me you are trying to get him to start drinking those terrible soda's that you call craft beer."

"Hey!," Arthur began, giving me a soft playful punch in the stomach. "But Josh is not wrong, Ben. They are bad."

"Come on dad, they were a hit back in college," Ben said with a smile. "Everyone wanted to try my line of craft beers."

"So it had the approval of college kids," I said with a chuckle and a shake of my head. "No wonder they liked it. They've never tried real beer..." Daisy tapped me on the shoulder, indicating the full beer glass she'd set on the bar beside me.

I plucked the glass up from the bar and offered it to Ben."...a real beer such as this one."

Ben gave Arthur a glance, and then turned back to me.

"I'm the designated driver. That's why I'm here, to drive my dad home after the parties over."

Arthur scoffed. "One beer won't hurt. And if it turns into two or more," he continued with a shrug, "we can simply call a cab."

Ben thought about it for a moment, before going 'oh well' and grabbed the proffered beer.

"Arthur, come on over here! I want you to meet Burt!"

Someone in our group yelled over the din, and waved Arthur over to them.

"I'll be right back," Arthur said, giving Ben a pat on the back, before striding off towards the still waving man.

"Guess the old man is still as popular as ever," Ben said with a grin as he shuffled over to stand at the bar beside me.

"Yep, he's one of the good ones. Sad to see him go." I said with a rueful nod.

Ben paused to take a sip of beer. He gave it an approving nod. "That's pretty good," he said, before turning his next words to me. "And how do you and my dad know each other?"

"He used to be my training officer years ago. Arthur taught me everything I know."

Ben nodded, silent for a long moment, as though contemplating something. "And does my dad know about...?" Ben raised his eyebrows, giving me a meaningful glance that I couldn't interpret.

"Know about?" I didn't bother to mask the confusion in my voice.

"Does he know that you're..." Ben glanced around as though we were about to be heard over the surrounding din. "...gay?"

My mind did a double take, surprised by the question. I was not sure where this was coming from — or how he'd even guessed my sexuality — so I answered evenly. "Yes, he does. Is that a problem for you?"

Ben paused a moment, a touch of confusion in his eyes, before he began stumbling over his words. “No! No, I don’t have a problem with it at all. Sorry, I’ve just realized how that sounded.” Ben sheepishly rubbed the back of his neck. “Look, I was going to mention it before, but I didn’t know if my dad knew.”

I sighed. I did not know where this conversation was going. But, I’d dealt with enough phobic assholes in my life to know there is no talking them round. And the last thing I wanted to do was to get into a fight with Ben at Arthur's retirement party.

I straightened up, and made to move away. “I need to go and check on...”

Ben raised his hands in a sign of apology. “Wait! I’m not judging! God, I’m doing this all wrong. Let me start again.” Ben took a long breath, and then dropped his hands and tucked them into his pockets. “I’m *B-Love24*.”

I blanked out for a few seconds, before clocking on.

This was the guy I’d messaged a couple times yesterday via the KissFerno dating app. That popular dating app was my mainstay method for finding hookups.

Except, on KissFerno, Ben’s profile had simply been a shirtless torso with his face cropped out. I, on the other hand, didn’t feel the need to hide away my features. I was more than happy to put my face on the line...so to speak.

At my lingering silence, Ben gave me a small unsure smile. “Very nice to meet you, *J-Heart3000*.”

I searched my memory, trying to think of a time when Arthur had ever mentioned his son was gay. But I was coming up blank.

“OK, well, I did not know that.” This was awkward. There was a reason why I used KissFerno to meet men — and didn’t bother going to Gay bars. Using technology let me keep my distance. And, with the bar scene, it is much too easy to stumble across a former fling. “Arthur never told me. But, good for you.” I said with a curt nod.

“Yeah, well, I just wanted to say. Actually, I’m not sure why I mentioned it,” Ben rubbed the back of his neck sheepishly. “I’m not even gay.”

At that new piece of information, all I could muster up was a single stony-faced raised eyebrow.

Chapter 2
BEN

'Ah, shit,' I chastised myself. *'What the heck am I doing?!'*

From the moment I set eyes on Josh, I immediately recognized him from his KissFerno profile. And I'd done a double-take when I saw him standing beside my father.

When my dad led me over to the guy, I was sure Josh would recognize me from the app.

It was a silly concern though. I had kept my face cropped out of the half-naked photo of my profile picture.

And I'd only gone onto KissFerno out of boredom, looking for a little fun. Although, admittedly, I was a little drunk at the time — at least a few beers in.

I meant to tick the box indicating that I was *'Straight'*, but I must have mis-clicked the box titled *'Gay'*. And I hadn't even noticed my mistake until an hour after my profile went live.

The first couple of men who sent me a 'Kiss' — to indicate their interest in me — should have been my first clue. And, at first, I put it down to them having misread my profile.

But, it wasn't until the fifteenth Kiss, that it occurred to me to go and double check my profile.

Opening up the app, I logged in, and there it was. Right beside my naked-chested picture — in bold caps — the word 'GAY MALE' came up as my sexual orientation.

It probably didn't help matters either, that my description read that I was *'up for anything'* and *'looking for someone nearby'*.

Now, I know I should have simply taken down the profile immediately. I should have deleted it — be glad my face wasn't on it — and called it a day.

But, then I received a Kiss from Josh. And what I saw of him turned my head. Even as a straight guy, I gotta admit, Josh was incredibly good-looking.

Between his firm muscled torso and big forearms, Josh stood out from all the other guys that had reached out to me.

Yet, it was the dimpled smile Josh wore in his profile picture, that captivated my attention.

That smile alone was what led me to inexplicably send Josh a Kiss back.

Unfortunately, standing in front of Josh in the real world, there was no trace of that dimpled smile looking down at me now.

Instead, all I saw was a tense frown punctuated by a cool gaze.

"And you go on dating apps to? What exactly?" Josh's voice was even. But, I could still hear the tense touch of annoyance in his tone. "You like to catfish and play games?"

"No, it's not like that." I tried not to rear back a little. There was a real intensity to Josh. And his huge muscled body added a powerful sense of presence that dwarfed my own.

I'd put my foot in it again.

It happened all the time whenever I got nervous around someone. Which led to me being terrible at picking up women.

Yet, as it turns out — even on the other end of the Kinsey scale — I'm still incredibly bad at turning on the charm.

But, damn it, I wanted to say the right thing to Josh. "It's a funny story actually." I paused with a chuckle.

Josh said nothing.

Awkwardly, I bumbled on, trying to break the tension. "I mean, it's kinda funny...at least once you hear it."

That was certainly not the right thing to say.

Josh waved me off. "No need to explain," he said, stony-faced. I wanted to see his dimpled smile, but had no idea how to do that.

I opened my mouth to say something, but then I heard my dad yell out. "Ben! Ben! Come on over here. I want you to meet these guys!"

I gave Josh a small apologetic smile — one which he did not reciprocate — and turned around to wave over at my dad. "I'll be right there!" I called out, before spinning back toward Josh.

Yet I was met with nothing but air. Josh had slipped away in the mere seconds it had taken for me to wave. And with a quick glance around the room, I found him already laughing it up with a group of men a little further down the bar.

Slumping my shoulders with a sigh, I turned back around and made my way over towards my dad.

Chapter 3
JOSH

It was well past midnight when the party finally began to wind down.

It had been a hoot — as friends both new and old — had dropped in at various times during the night to wish Arthur well.

I'd personally down a heck of a lot of beer, but still didn't feel tipsy. Instead, I simply felt a bit of a buzz. Yet, it was enough to let me know that I was not going to be driving home tonight.

So, I ordered a cab instead. And standing just outside the bar entrance archway, I took in the deep crisp air of the night.

While I waited, my fellow party stragglers wandered out of the bar. And as each one of them past me, I nodded my final good nights to them, as they made their way home.

I was all smiles, until I saw Ben wander out through the doors of the bar.

I gave him a stiff, but polite, nod of my head. "Goodnight then."

Ben moved to stand a little aways from me, but didn't move much further. Instead, to my slight annoyance, he leaned back against the brick wall on the other side of the archway.

Tucking his hands into his pockets, Ben made a show of shivering. "Doesn't feel all that good."

I grunted with a noncommittal sound as I turned away to look down the road.

"I mean, it's warmer in my college state. Not that much warmer, but it's different, you know?"

"Mm." My reply was as terse as I felt.

"I'm waiting for a cab to come and pick up dad and me." With my head turned away from him, Ben did not see my eyes roll back as he continued with this strained one-sided conversation. "I was only going to have one drink. But every one of dad's friends kept offering me a beer, so..."

"Um hmm." My jaw tensed with annoyance.

"Anyway, I've had a few too many. But it was still a great shindig. So, you waiting for a cab too?"

"Yup." I didn't bother to expand on my single word answer. Instead, I peered down at the toe of my boot, taking a moment to rub it to a shine against the back of my pants leg.

"That's great!" Ben's voice brightened at the news.

Curious, I relented, and finally peered over at Ben. And the earnestness in his eyes would've been endearing, if I wasn't still pissed off about our earlier encounter.

After our conversation, I'd made a point of carefully avoiding Ben for the rest of the night. And — I'm not ashamed to admit that — I was worried he'd whip out his phone, and pull up my profile. Only to then show it off to Arthur and everyone else.

"...we should all share a cab." Ben's enthusiasm didn't wane in the face of the return of my stony silence. "It'll be better than waiting all night for your cab to arrive."

"I live on the other side of town from Arthur. Eastside." I answered, feeling my iciness begin to melt a touch in the face of Ben's genuinely warm personality.

"Oh," Ben's shoulders dipped a little, making him appear very much like a sad puppy. I bit back the touch of a grin that threatened to reach my lips. "Guess sharing the cab doesn't make sense. But, the Eastside is rough. You like it there?"

I shrugged. "Was born and raised there my whole life. It can get rough at times, but that's why I stay near. That way I can help out my friends and neighbors at a drop of a hat."

Ben nodded at my answer with a broad smile. "You really are a man with a heart of gold, huh."

I scoffed. "Staying where you grew up is hardly worthy of a medal."

"It's not about the staying, it's about why you stayed. God, it's cold." Ben pulled his hands from his pockets, and crossed them, tucking his hands into his armpits. "You stayed for your family and friends. To keep them safe."

I nodded. "Yeah well," I shuffled my weight from one foot to the other. "Someone has too."

The quiet that followed that statement felt tense, punctuated only by the faint sounds of traffic rumbling past on the nearby main street.

It was Ben who finally broke the silence.

"I'm sorry about before, when I sprung all of that KissFerno stuff on you."

I waved him off. "Don't worry about it."

"No, it needs to be said." Glancing over at him, I found Ben staring down at his shoes as he continued. "I made a mistake on my profile, but I didn't pick up on it until much later. I wasn't cat-fishing you, or anything like that."

I raised an eyebrow when Ben finally raised his eyes to meet mine. "You don't need to explain yourself to me," I told him with all sincerity. "Online dating was how I first jumped into the gay scene years ago."

Ben shook his head fervently. "Seriously, I wasn't kidding before. I really am straight."

His voice sounded so sincere, that I really didn't know who Ben was trying to convince — myself or him.

If Ben was this deep in the closet, then I wasn't going to pry that door open. No matter how hot I thought he was.

'Damn it, Josh. Ben's strictly off limits as a hookup...no matter what his pretty eyes do to you.' I scolded myself. *'Arthur would kill me.'*

Besides, Ben would figure himself out in time, just like I did when I was in my mid twenties.

When I opened my mouth to assure Ben that I believed him, I was interrupted by the short sharp sound of a car horn. Turning towards the noise, I saw a cab roll to a stop outside the bar.

The cab driver leaned towards the opened passenger seat window of his vehicle. "I'm here to pickup Josh Wright?"

I nodded at the cab driver. "That's me," I answered, then twisted round to give Ben a mock-salute. "You and the old man get home safe, yah hear?"

Ben grinned, mirth coloring his eyes. "Goodnight, Josh"

And with that, I made my way into the cab, and relaxed back into the seat with an exhausted sigh.

Chapter 4
BEN

When the words on the page started to blur, I relented and finally took a break.

It was already well into the early evening, some eight hours after I'd started studying for the day.

But coursework waits for no-one. And my final year of pre-med was absolutely swamping me with it.

This weekend break from my college campus, was a chance to catchup with my folks, and go to my dad's retirement party. But, I still had too much work to get through. So, my stack of textbooks simply came along with me.

Shoving back the open textbook, I yawned as I rubbed away the dryness from my eyes. I was still feeling dehydrated from all the beer I'd drunk last night.

Sat at a small desk, in the guest room of my parents new home, I eased back into my chair and blew out a breath.

My parents had bought this house — downsizing our old family home — as soon as I'd left for college.

The house was modest, but still quaint, and it was situated on the edge of the Northside district. And it was the perfect place for my folks to live out their retirement years.

But, there wasn't a lot to do around here. And I didn't know any of the local neighbors.

On one hand, this distraction free environment meant that I could get caught up on a bunch of studying. But, it also meant there wasn't much to do if I needed to unwind afterwards.

My phone buzzed, startling me for a moment as it hummed atop the desk.

Picking up my phone, I was surprised to find a notification alerting me to a KissFerno message from *J-Heart3000.*

I unlocked my phone, and went straight into the dating app. But, at the last second I paused with my finger hovered over the 'read message' button.

I was really curious to see what Josh had sent. But, if I checked it, would that mean I was messing around with the guy?

Last night — after my dad and I finally left the bar — I made a promise to myself that I would delete my profile first thing in the morning.

But, as soon as I got back home, I went straight upstairs and collapsed onto the bed fast asleep. And the next morning I was so absorbed by my coursework, it had completely slipped my mind.

Until now.

'Still, Josh messaged me, not the other way around.' I thought to myself. *'It would be impolite not to at least read his message. Right?'*

And with that thought, I tapped open Josh's message.

#J-Heart3000: Hey, B. Just reaching out to say sorry for the way I acted last night. I was a bit of an ass, didn't mean to push. Hope you are well. J

It took me a long moment to notice that I was wearing a broad smile on my face, as I reread Josh's message for a third time.

It felt strange, acting all giddy over another guy's simple apology.

But, despite his gruff demeanor towards me last night, there was something warm and inviting about the way Josh interacted with his crowd of friends at the party. And it made me want to get to know him better.

Or maybe I was simply feeling a little lonely — *and a lot bored* — and Josh messaging me was a great distraction.

So, setting all of my doubts aside, I opted to send Josh a message back.

 # B-Love2424: Its ok, we r cool. I wd hv been pissed bout it 2. U get home safe?

After tapping 'send', I placed my phone back onto the desk. And with a sigh I returned my attention back towards my textbook.

The words still blurred.

As I began to lightly slap my cheeks to re-energize myself, my phone buzzed again.

Picking my phone back up, to my mild shock, it was another message from Josh!

This time I didn't hesitate. It seemed like Josh was available for a quick messaging conversation. And I was more than happy to ignore my textbook, so that I could instead focus on Josh.

 # J-Heart3000: Yes I did. Thanks for asking. And glad we are cool again. You should let me buy you another beer one day as a proper apology. You never got to finish the first one I gave you.

Reading through the long message, I grinned. Seemed like Josh was much more chatty via text than in real-life.

That message was the longest string of words I'd gotten out of Josh since he found out I was B-Love2424.

I quickly typed in my reply.

 # B-Love2424: Y not buy me that beer right now?

I tapped 'send' before I stopped to think about it.

'Wait a second. Does that make me look like I'm coming onto him or something?' I hurriedly tapped out a followup message. I didn't want to give Josh the wrong idea.

 # B-Love2424: I need a brk frm studying. Brain melting. Need to unwind. :) You'd b doing me a favor.

I tapped the send button with a nod. *'That should clear things up. And if Josh doesn't reply back, well, then I could...'*

My train of thought was interrupted by the notification buzz going off.

 # J-Heart3000: I know a place. Send me your number and I'll text you the details.

Chapter 5
JOSH

For the third time in a row, Ben sank the black ball into the pocket in a single smooth long shot, winning the game.

"Yes!" Ben raised his hands triumphantly as I watched on bemused. Dropping his pool cue onto the table, he then made a show of taking a bow. "The cue-master reigns undefeated!"

I chuckled, placing my beer down on the edge of the pool table, and began an appreciative clap. "Well done."

"And...?" Ben cupped a hand around his ear as he tilted his head towards me as though encouraging me to speak up.

I rubbed my brow and sighed. "And the cue-master reigns undefeated..." I then rolled my eyes when Ben began to literally pat himself on the back. "...and who is clearly the most gracious opponent to ever play the game," I continued drolly.

Ben and I were in one of my favorite sports bars in the Eastside. And it was the first place that came to mind when Ben told me that he needed to unwind.

Other than the station, this place was pretty much my home away from home. It was a great place to relax after work, when I wanted to do something a little more than simply down a beer.

And right now, it was nice and quiet, with only a few patrons downing a few drinks, before the late-evening rush kicked in.

This place was neutral ground, and I never brought any of my hookups here.

And yet, (when Ben had arrived at the bar 30 minutes after I'd messaged him with the location), I felt a little bit excited. It felt silly, but I really wanted to impress Ben.

So, that is where my suggestion of a game of pool came in.

I'm not too modest to admit that I am a pretty decent pool player, easily beating all of the other guys back at the station. But, despite all the hours I'd put in at the pool table, Ben had trounced me three games in a row.

"If I'd known you were this good at pool, I would have picked a different game, like darts," I said as I jutted my chin over at the dartboard on the wall opposite. "Unless, of course, you're a crack shot at that too?" I wondered aloud.

Ben grinned. "Naw, pool is my hidden talent. I managed to pay for a lot of my textbooks betting against my friends at the pool table, in the college rec room."

"I don't doubt it," I said as I snagged my beer off the table, and stepped back to give Ben room to rack up another game.

Ben hummed in agreement. "I wasn't any good at football or athletics back in high school," Ben continued as he set about placing the pool balls into the rack. "Phys Ed wasn't my thing. But, once I got to college, I finally discovered my natural talent," Ben tapped his hand lightly on the green felt. "I find pool easier, because it's all about judging the angles, not cardio."

"With all of that college work, I'm surprised you've had the time to do anything else in your downtime," I said as I moved to pick up my pool cue. I then chuckled as I continued, "...other than making craft soda beers, of course."

Ben made a show of looking affronted, then cracked a smile. "You're never going to let that one go, are you." Ben then paused, thoughtfully tilting his head. "I needed an outlet to blow off steam, and pool works for me. Plus, I made a few bucks extra to help pay for all of my brewing ingredients. I guess you could say that pool helps me to make the *best* damn tasting beers in the world."

Ben stared pointedly at me with a single raised eyebrow, daring me to contradict him. But, I merely shrugged and raised my palms into the air in surrender.

"Sure, whatever you say." I grinned.

"Yeah, that's right." Ben returned my grin with a nod, and then grabbed his cue. He then strode around the table, and made his way over to the other end where I stood. "Pool is pretty much my third favorite thing to do in life...so the cue-master was born."

I shuffled back a couple steps to give Ben room to lean over the table and take his shot. It was then that I noticed Ben's firm jean-clad ass was right in my face.

It was firm, round, and altogether much too juicy for me to ignore. I tried to tear my eyes away from it, but I was transfixed.

'Damn,' I thought, when the sound of pool balls clacking finally woke me from my wet-daydream.

I quickly angled my eyes away as Ben turned around, and prayed that he hadn't noticed me leering. *'Damn it!'* I repeated the thought, cursing myself at almost having been caught.

My mind flashed with the image from Ben's dating app profile. Ben's face had been cropped out, but he'd hidden nothing of his naked torso, showing off his lean but well-defined muscle.

I clenched my jaw, and shook my head as though to shake away the memory of Ben's lickable abs.

Ben was straight, (or at least that's the story he was going with). Besides, he was Arthur's family. So, there was no chance I was going to try and hookup with him.

'Put that thought right out of your mind. Right Now!' I chastised myself.

"Hey? Josh?" Ben was waving a hand in my face, shaking me from my reverie. "You're up."

"Um, yup," I gave him a curt nod and quickly moved around him — careful not to brush up against his firm body — and then leaned down to take my shot.

And completely missed.

'Damn it,' I cursed myself again. My lusty thoughts of Ben had distracted me.

I seriously needed to get my mind off of this line of thinking. And that's when I remembered Ben's earlier divulgence. "What's your first thing?" I said as I moved out of the way to let Ben take his shot.

But, this time I was careful to keep his delicious ass out of my direct line of sight.

"Huh? First thing?" Ben took his shot smoothly, and the ball sunk right down into the pocket. And yet Ben was already moving around the table to get into position for his next shot.

I leaned against my cue as I watched the self-acclaimed cue-master work his magic once again.

"You said pool is your third favorite thing to do in your downtime," I clarified, shaking my head as Ben somehow managed to sink two pool balls off a single shot. "I'm guessing brewing beers is your favorite past-time?"

"Brewing? Naw. That's only second place," Ben answered as he hustled around the pool table again.

It took me a moment too long to realize that Ben was leaning over the table right in front of me. And it wasn't until my eyes again drifted down to his firm ass, that I remembered why I needed to keep a little distance.

Worse still, I could even feel my manhood begin to twitch with excitement at the sight of Ben leaning down over the table.

"So, what's the first thing?" I repeated, genuinely curious as to what Ben's answer would be.

As he straightened, Ben pivoted around to face me, but we were both now stood a little too close.

The corner spot of the bar — where the large pool table was — didn't really leave much room for us to maintain a respectable distance.

Ben fell silent as he carefully eyed me, and I noticed an unmistakable dilation of his pupils, and a touch of heat to his cheeks. And my eyes drifted down to find Ben's tongue sneaking out to wet his lips.

We stood like that for a long tense heated moment, and I could feel the front of my pants begin to tighten.

'Not now!' I thought as I hurriedly turned away. Quickly stepping around Ben, I cleared my throat while I tried to surreptitiously adjust my dick. But the brush of my hand, across the front of my pants, only made my cock stand to attention even more.

I needed to keep a bit of distance from Ben — just for a little bit — until I managed to calm my body down.

"Well, I guess coursework has to be your favorite thing right now." I tried to brush off the uncomfortable moment, angling my body slightly away from Ben who still stood stock still where I'd left him. He hadn't even turned round to face me as I spoke, but I continued talking anyway. "No choice, I suppose. That's simply the way it is when your studying something tough like medicine, right?" *Why was I rambling? What the hell was happening?* "Final year of pre-med must be tough."

Ben hummed a noncommittal sound as — with his back still towards me — he hustled around the table. It was strange to watch him awkwardly shuffle to the other side of the table like that. "Yeah it is," Ben answered, casting me an uncomfortable glance over his shoulder. "All of that studying. So tough. But, hey, are those bathrooms?" Ben rushed out the words. Confused, I wordlessly watched as he paced off in the direction of the nearest bathroom. "I'll be right back."

And with that, Ben was gone.

Chapter 6

BEN

"*What the hell are you doing!*" I stage-whispered down at my dick, as I ran a frustrated hand through my hair.

Striding into the thankfully empty bathroom, I'd shut myself off into one of the empty cubicles.

When Josh had asked me about my number one favorite pastime, memory's of past sexual encounters flashed across my mind.

So, when I turned around to face him, I was getting ready to make a joke about getting laid. In particular, one memory of a pretty sweet blow job I got from an ex, had come to mind.

But, looking up into Josh's warm brown eyes, the image of my ex-girlfriend was suddenly replaced by an image of Josh. And all I could imagine was him giving me that blow job instead.

If that wasn't bad enough, that very vivid image had put my dick on full alert. And my well-fitted jeans did nothing to hide that fact.

There was no way I could turn around to face Josh with my obvious excitement on clear display. So I'd jogged in here like a frickin' idiot, slammed myself into a cubicle, and then tried to chastise my dick back into line.

It had been a couple minutes, and talking to my dick wasn't working. *"Why in the hell are you getting hard over this guy?"* I briefly considered quickly rubbing one out. Yet, I wasn't ready for that. Jacking off was one thing, but jacking off while imagining that it was Josh's firm hands gripped around my cock, was quite another.

If talking it down wasn't going to work, then I was going to have to think of something else completely.

Closing my eyes, I brought to mind images from my textbooks. When it came to pre-med, my textbooks often contained some really gross pictures of every gruesome medical condition imaginable.

After an extra minute of memory recall — including one specific picture of a diseased colon, that had pretty much scarred me for life — it worked.

My dick was finally back under control.

'For now,' I thought grimly, when I unlocked the cubicle door.

As I made my way back over to the pool table, Josh wasn't there. However, as I let my eyes wander over the bar, I soon found Josh standing over by the front window beside the entrance.

Making my way over, I noticed how intently he stared out that window, clearly focused on something across the street.

"Hey, anything good out there?... Woah!" I startled when Josh's head snapped around, as he dragged his intense gaze away from the window.

Josh seemed to do a double take before recognizing me. He then relaxed. "Sorry about that," Josh said, already turning his attention back out the window. "I know that guy. He's a perp I read about in a recent case." I watched silently as Josh tilted his head in thought. "I think he might be able to lead me to the others."

"Which others?" I asked, confused over this sudden change in Josh's demeanor. A little over five minutes ago, we were having drinks and playing pool. Next thing I know, Josh's talking about cases and perps.

Josh angled his attention away from the window with a grimace. "Look, I'm sorry to have to do this, but can we take a rain check?"

"Wait, what? Why?"

"I have to follow that guy." Josh was already making his way back over to the pool table. I hurried after him as I watched him snag up his jacket from off the nearby chair we'd rested our jackets on. "He has ties to a crew that has been peddling methamphetamines around the Eastside. You can call a cab to take you home, right?" Josh said, giving me a quick pat on the shoulder. And then he stepped around me to make his way out.

"Hold up!" I grabbed my own jacket from the chair, and jogged after him.

Josh's long strides already put him at the entryway, his hand on the door handle. But I quickly caught up, and placed a palm on his upper arm to stop him. Something which was very much to his annoyance, if the look on his face was anything to go by.

I was a little surprised that the mere weight of my hand on his arm had brought him to a stop. Josh could have easily shrugged me off and carried on. "Come on, Josh, I only popped to the bathroom. Now you're running out on me?"

Josh's tight expression eased. "I'm not running out on you," he paused when I gave him a dubious look, and then corrected himself. "OK, fine. Yes, I am. But, it's for a good reason. And I'll tell you about it later tonight." With that, he snatched open the door, and made his way out.

I jogged after him, not liking how it felt being brushed off. "Seriously, what's going on?" I asked as Josh quickly covered the short distance to his car parked a little ways down from the bar.

I hurried around to the passenger side as soon as Josh remotely unlocked the doors of his vehicle. And before he could stop me, I snatched open the car door.

"Seriously?" Josh gave me an annoyed glance from where he stood over on the drivers side. "I can't give you a lift right now."

Honestly, I couldn't figure out why it was so important for me to stay near Josh. I mean, just a few minutes ago, I was walking at speed — *and definitely not running* — away from him because I didn't want him to see my boner.

And now there was nowhere else I'd rather be.

So we both stood there, each one holding our respective car doors open, as we stared each other down across the bonnet.

It was a tense few seconds. And just when I was about to give up and raise my hands in surrender, Josh sighed.

I grinned as I watched the man rub his face in frustration. "Fine, get in the damn car. I'll tell you about it on the way."

Chapter 7
JOSH

This was a bad idea.

My hands tightened around the handles of my long distance camera, and the shutter rapidly clicked when I took a few more photos.

Peering through the lens, I readjusted the distance of my shot, as a few men gathered outside of the all-night laundromat down the street.

I'd parked my car a good distance away — carefully keeping the car lights off as I did — so I could stay as incognito as possible.

And beside me, his body seemingly thrumming with excitement, sat Ben.

As soon as I agreed to let Ben ride along with me, I immediately regretted the decision.

'I should not have brought him with me,' I thought, mentally kicking myself.

But when I told Ben to get in the car, it was out of a sense of urgency. I had no time to waste as, out of the corner of my eye, I could already see the perp climbing onto his motorcycle.

That's why I had no choice. *'Yeah, keep telling yourself that,'* I thought to myself with a grimace, as I shuttered a few more pictures of gang members outside the laundromat. *'It's certainly not because you kinda like having Ben around.'*

"Are we going to go in?"

My hands tightened a touch more. So much so, that I almost thought I would end up cracking my camera's casing.

Ben's voice had suddenly filled out the long stretched out silence. And his question made me feel a touch on edge, and very much off-balance.

I've done plenty of these low-key off-duty stakeouts on my own. And each time, I maintained a strict routine of silence, while I observed whichever perp I was trailing.

My police captain didn't know I did these stakeouts. And for good reason, since I know my captain would take me off a case if he ever found out. But, doing this work off-hours meant I could gather the extra evidence I needed to move forward on a case and close it.

And, it sounds crazy, but I found them kind of relaxing. Some people do Yoga to meditate. I, on the other hand, do off-duty stakeouts to help find my inner calm.

Still, going the extra mile is what made me damn good at my job. Nevertheless, it also made it difficult to hold down a relationship. Especially when I would have to explain why I was skipping out on a date.

'Kind of like today's non-date with Ben,' I thought to myself.

"No, we are not going in. I'm simply gathering a bit of information. That is all," I said aloud as I placed the camera down onto the dashboard with a shrug. "On the drive over here, I told you it was going to be boring."

"You also said that this guy you needed to follow was in a motorcycle gang." Ben stated as he leaned forward in his seat. I grinned when Ben squinted, as though he were trying to get a better look at the gang members way down the street. He was never going to get a clear view, not from this distance. "Does that camera..." Ben jutted a chin at the camera in front of me. "...get a good enough picture from this range?"

"Yes it does, and for good reason. It let's me keep my distance. Remember again how I said that this is simply an information-gathering mission?" I paused, waiting long enough for Ben to notice and angle his attention to me.

"Yup. You said — and I quote," Ben cleared his throat and put on a comically deep voice. "*I am Josh-man. I am vengeance. I find the bad guys, and no-one will get in my way.*"

I pinched the bridge of my nose, biting the side of my cheek to stop the grin threatening to spread across my face.

"I did not say that." My tone was as even and no-nonsense as I could make it. "I said that I have a job to do. And that you could come along if you stayed in the car, and stayed silent."

Ben waved me off. "So, I was paraphrasing. Potato, Po-tah-toe. So..." Ben brightened, his brows raised high on his head in excitement. "Are we going to go in guns ablaze?"

I gave him an incredulous look. "Aren't you the son of a cop?" I shook my head, as I looked him up and down. "What do you think we do all day?"

Ben shrugged. "Dad never really let me into his world when it comes to all of this." Ben waved in the direction of the laundromat, which still had a few men milling around outside. The small initial group of three gang members had now increased to a group of ten.

That was interesting enough to make me reach for my camera again.

"Arthur never took you on a ride along?" I asked, as I snapped a few more photos.

"Not once. Although I think that was more my mom's insistence, than anything." Ben shifted around in his seat a little. "Although, sitting still for hours on end is not my thing. My butts getting numb like this."

I lowered the camera. "We've been here for less than an hour. I've done longer stretches sat on the john."

Ben chuckled. "Then you really need to eat more fiber." I rolled my eyes, then returned my attention towards the gathering at the laundromat. "And I've been sat for a lot longer today," Ben continued, shifting around a little more before finally finding a relaxing position. "I did a six plus hours long study stretch. Although I do regret not taking a few more breaks."

I'd taken all of the pictures I would take of this batch of loitering gang members, so I returned my camera onto it's dashboard resting place.

"If you keep studying hard non-stop like that, you're gonna burn yourself out," I told Ben, my words sounding strangely reminiscent of Arthur's warning to me yesterday.

Maybe Arthur was right, and I needed to dial down the intensity I had for my work.

"You sound like my dad." Ben's reply made me snap my head around. It were as though he'd read my mind.

"How so?"

Ben shrugged. "He thinks I work too hard too. Constantly asking me when I'm going to do something other than study, and finally bring home a girlfriend to meet the folks."

I cracked a smile. Seems like Arthur was badgering Ben with pretty much the same warnings about life as he did with me. And then Ben's words hit me. "So, is that why you were on the app? Looking for a girl to finally bring home to mom and dad?" I tried to keep my tone light, punctuating my words with a cocky grin. But I could hear the slight edge to my voice.

It did not work, because Ben fell silent for a moment too long for the typically talkative guy. And his blue eyes seemed to search my expression for something.

I fought the urge to explain my joke — explain that I wasn't accusing him of cat-fishing again — but I stayed silent while Ben's unreadable gaze bore into me.

And then the moment was all of a sudden over.

Ben's shoulders slumped, as he turned his gaze down and away from my own. "That's not what I was on there for." He sighed, sounding almost defeated. But defeated by what, I had no clue. "I was looking for something, I don't know, someone. Maybe have some fun, and see where it would lead from there." He then raised his eyes back up to meet mine, a curious challenge hidden behind his captivating orbs. "What were you looking for on KissFerno? I mean..." Ben reached up to rub the back of his neck, as he continued. "...what do you want when you're checking out a guy?"

My mouth went dry at the question.

I tamped down the urge to zero in on Ben's lips. Especially when, from the periphery of my vision, I could see Ben wet them again. And the flicker of his tongue caused my cock to flicker with excitement.

'Don't tell him,' I silently warned myself. If this wasn't the confirmation I needed that Ben was more than a little bi-curious, I didn't know what was. *'Don't say that you want him.'*

If any other man had asked me that, I would have made a flirtatious pass. This would have been the moment I'd move in, closing the space between us, until I was close enough to simply lean in for a kiss.

And then from there, we'd take it further — *a lot further* — until my body finally got the release it damn well deserved.

Yet, out of respect to my former training officer and friend, I couldn't make a move on Ben like that.

But, before either Ben or I said another word, loud shouting suddenly broke the silence.

The yelling was coming from the direction of the laundromat. And, snatching up my camera, I peered through the long lens to get a clear view of what was happening.

The group of men now appeared to be gathered around two from their group who were now brawling it out.

The fight looked more drunken than wild. Yet the energy of the anger between the two fighters was starting to ripple through the group.

A couple of the men that had formed a loose ring around the two brawlers were now beginning to shove one another.

Within a minute — almost like a chain reaction that was lit by the fire of the initial fight — all of the ten or so strong group were now duking it out.

I briefly considered calling it in. But I also knew that I would have to explain how I'd managed to stumble across the brawl — in the middle of the night — in the first place.

And that was a conversation with my police captain that I did *not* want to have tomorrow morning.

My thoughts were interrupted by a low *'thump, thump, thump'* in the car. And the sound was just loud enough to be heard over the shouting going on outside.

Angling my eyes towards the direction of the thumping, I found Ben's heel tapping repeatedly against the floor, as he rapidly jiggled his knee.

Looking over at Ben, I could see him leaning forward in his seat, enrapt by the scene happening down the street. He was squinting again, trying to get a good look. But, Ben's rapid heel let me know he was more than a little nervous right now.

I reached out and placed a hand on Ben's thigh, stilling his jittery leg. The physical touch brought Ben's attention to me. And, without thinking, I gave his thigh a comforting squeeze.

To my surprise, this didn't seem to bother him. In fact, he seemed thankful for the calming touch. "Sorry, I'm just excited about all of this. I'm on a dangerous all night stakeout, with a gang fight happening down the street."

"This is hardly an all night stakeout," I said with a quick glance at the dashboard clock. I was caught off guard when it read 1:16am. I hadn't even noticed the time go by.

I thought being in the car with Ben by my side would be an awkward stilted affair. But, it turns out, that being around him was comfortable. Fun even.

In fact, this is probably the most fun I've had — *with my clothes on, of course* — with a guy I met off a dating app.

It was then that I noticed that my hand was still resting on Ben's thigh. Yet he didn't seem to notice or appear bothered by it.

I lifted my hand slowly off his leg, immediately regretting it when I could no longer feel the heat of his thigh under my palm.

"Well, I think this is our cue to go." The yelling outside had begun to die down, and I had everything I'd come here to get. I used the noise of the men shouting to cover the start of my engine. And, keeping the car headlights off, I shifted out of park.

"Yeah, well, indulge me anyway." Ben smiled warmly, relaxing back into his seat as I reversed the vehicle. "When anyone asks what I did this break, this will have been a dangerous stakeout."

I scoffed as I did a three-point-turn in the middle of the utterly empty street. "I would never bring you to somewhere where you'd get hurt." There was just enough flickering streetlight for me to make the maneuver without headlights. "Besides, Arthur would kill me." I dead-panned.

"I know," Ben agreed. "Still, I was ready to give you back up, if you had to take down those dudes."

We turned a corner, taking us back onto the main street, which was still fairly busy at such an early hour of the morning.

"You really think you could have taken on those men, huh?" I let my eyes briefly rake over Ben, as I remembered the image of his muscular torso.

I didn't bother to hide the appreciative look on my face as Ben's photo appeared in my minds eye.

But I then quickly shook the lascivious thoughts from my mind, bringing me back into the moment. "It doesn't matter either way." My hands tightened around the steering wheel as I refocused my entire attention on the road ahead of me. "This isn't a buddy cop movie. You can't go rushing into things. Not if you want it to hold up in court."

I could feel the heat of Ben's eyes on the side of my face. "You certainly look like you could hold your own anyway, if you had to fight." Ben said appreciably as he loosely gripped my bicep. His hand didn't even reach half-way around my arm. "Pretty firm."

He kept his hand there, long enough that I glanced over at him. And what I saw in his eyes almost made me stop the car, and pull him into a kiss right then and there.

His eyes were filled with expectation, the kind I'd seen on the faces of the many men in my past who'd wanted to jump into my bed.

I could feel my cock thicken in excitement, ready and eager to be touched and sucked. And it took everything in my power to tear my eyes away from Ben's and reaffix my gaze onto the road.

"I'll drop you off home." My voice was tight, the words forced through my clenched jaw.

And at my words, Ben let go of my bicep, and returned to rest his hand on his thigh.

I needed to put a bit more of a respectable space between us before I did something I'd regret.

Ben sighed. "Fine, but can we at least stop off for takeout. I'm starving."

I grimaced at the thought of the various greasy takeouts, (that I knew of locally), that still stayed open this late. None of them were the kind of place that I'd eat from.

And so — *in a moment of madness and against my better judgment* — I blurted out my bright idea.

"I'll cook you something back at my place," I said, glancing over to find Ben looking back at me with mild surprise.

Ben quickly brightened. "Sure, let's go to yours."

Chapter 8
BEN

It didn't take long to reach Josh's apartment. But the entire drive over felt thrilling, and the air was thick with anticipation.

This was it.

I had no idea how far I was going to go tonight, but the tension between Josh and myself was palpable.

I've never slept with a guy before, not even kissed a man. But, I have been curious in the past. But that curiosity only went as far as the odd lingering glance over at a buff guy on college campus. Or sometimes the odd towel-clad dude wandering out of the shared dormitory showers.

But now it seemed like I was about to experience my first sexual encounter with a man, and I was thrumming with nerves.

So, as soon as Josh invited me into his nicely kept open-plan home, I quickly began to ready myself for the next step.

Snatching off my jacket, I tossed it onto the couch, and then turned on my heel to face him. But — to my complete and utter puzzlement — Josh had wandered off over to the kitchen area.

"So, you want a grilled cheese?"

I wordlessly gaped at Josh.

After a long pregnant pause, he must have clearly read the confusion on my face, because he repeated his question.

"Grilled cheese? You want any, or no?"

He waved the spatula in his hand to indicate the frying pan on the cooker. "It's pretty much the only thing I can cook," Josh said with a shrug as he glanced around his kitchen. "But you can rest assured that it'll be cooked in a clean kitchen."

It took a moment longer, but I finally found my voice. "Dude, are you for real right now?"

Josh cocked his head at me in an almost comical look of confusion. "What do you mean? I cleaned my kitchen just this morning."

"I'm not talking about the kitchen." I paused to blow out a frustrated breath and then ran a hand across my face. "I wasn't talking about the kitchen, or the grilled cheese. I'm talking about all of this." I waved my hands around to indicate the apartment. "Why did you really bring me back here?"

Josh stared me down, his face expressionless for a long moment, before he too blew out a breath that sounded as frustrated as I felt.

"I don't know what you mean." Josh said as he dropped the spatula onto the kitchen countertop behind him. He then leaned back against the countertop.

As he folded his arms, I took in the powerful show of Josh's bulging muscles. They underpinned a huge chest that almost looked like it could pop open the buttons of his tight fitting shirt.

"Look..." I began as I moved across the room to stand in front of him. My fingers itched to reach out for Josh, but I wasn't sure if my touch would be welcome.

Not knowing what to do with my hands, I tucked them into my pockets as I continued. "I've been getting vibes from you all night. And I don't know how you guys do this..."

"*You* guys?" Josh gave me a questioning raised brow.

I rolled my eyes. "I simply meant that I'm not sure how gay guys hit on guys." I deadpanned before continuing in a normal tone. "But I've been getting a sense that you want me."

"Not every gay man in the world is out to seduce you." Josh said, dropping his crossed arms with a scoff.

I ran a frustrated hand through my hair, racking my brain to try to find the right words, before realizing that I didn't need to.

Josh had just given me an idea — *I would seduce him.*

As Josh stared me down I firmly held his gaze as I slowly pulled up the hem of my shirt, dragging the material up to display my tight abs.

I might not have been ready to voice out loud what I wanted from Josh. But, I was for damn sure, going to show him what he could have if he made the next move.

We stood facing each other in tense silence — Josh's eyes transfixed on my gaze — as I raised my other hand up to rest it on the back of my head.

Tucking my shirt up a little higher, I let my palm run slowly across my bare stomach. And I bit back a grin at the sight of Josh's eyes flaring up with a wanton look I instantly recognized.

His eyes, however, no longer met mine. Instead, his gaze now was fastened on the movement of my hand across my exposed body.

I held my breath as Josh blew out a growl of frustration, as he tore his eyes away from my body, angling his gaze away to the floor.

I openly grinned now, knowing that I was finally starting to break down the control of this tightly wound man.

Dropping my hand down from my head, I reached out and grasped Josh's hand. And I reveled in the feel of his firm digits as I guided them up towards my lips.

Josh said nothing when I briefly kissed his work-roughened fingertips. And, as I carefully watched Josh, I could tell from his tightly clenched jaw that he was still fighting himself.

I wanted to feel his hands on me, especially now that I could feel my burgeoning erection begin to grow harder and more urgent.

So, I wordlessly guided Josh's hand down towards my bare abs.

I continued to hold up the material of my shirt, loving how Josh's transfixed eyes intently watched me move his hand.

But, he did not pull away as I gently moved his palm across my stomach. And I bit back a thrill at the feel of his rough fingers moving across my skin.

But I needed more. I needed Josh to take control, to show me that he wanted me as much as I wanted him.

After a few more long seconds of silence, the excitement of his hand on my body quickly began to fade.

Josh wasn't taking control as I'd hoped he would — *he was giving me nothing!*

He hadn't pulled away, hadn't chastised me, or uttered a word of disgust.

But maybe a semi-strip tease wasn't how Josh got his rocks off. And all I was doing was acting like a fool in front of him.

'God, this is ridiculous,' I silently chastised myself. I could feel my cheeks burning with embarrassment as I took a half-step back. I dropped Josh's hand, and it fell limply to his side.

Yet the movement seemed to shock Josh out of a stupor, as I watched him gaze back up at me, his eyes meeting my own in surprise.

Straightening my shirt, I shrugged helplessly, an apology already on my lips.

"I shouldn't have done..." I began, just as Josh took a step forward, and reached up to grasp either side of my face.

And before I knew what was happening, he was pulling me into a kiss.

Chapter 9
JOSH

His mouth tasted even better than I'd imagined.

I inhaled Ben in, my tongue pushing in to meet his. Our bodies stood flush against one another, and I could feel Ben's own hard cock pressing against my own firm manhood.

I'd been mesmerized by his abs, fighting to keep every muscle in my body from trembling with need.

However, from the moment Ben placed my hand on his firm muscled abs, I'd been fighting it, trying not to give in. And yet the moment Ben let go of my hand, the loss of the heat of his touch was too much.

I needed to feel him again. *I wanted to feel him again.*

And as we desperately kissed, I let my hands drift down from Ben's face, down his back, to cup his round firm butt cheeks in the palm of my hands.

I brought him impossibly closer to me with a low growl, before leaning back to break off our kiss.

Smiling, I took in his round blown pupils — sat in the middle of two crystal blue orbs — as Ben looked hopefully up at me.

"Let's take this into the bedroom."

"Thank God," Ben quickly answered, his eyes drifting back down to look hungrily at my lips. "I thought you'd never ask."

With a chuckle, I removed my hands from Ben's ass and grabbed his hand, leading him off towards my bedroom.

I briefly debated picking him up and carrying him over my shoulder into the room, but quickly shut that thought down.

I was horny, for sure. But, I don't think Ben was quite ready for me to go all gay caveman on him just yet.

Once we entered my bedroom, I guided him over towards my bed, our eyes never leaving each other, as he back peddled towards the edge of the bed.

I made quick work of his shirt, unbuttoning and removing it even before he fell back onto the mattress. And Ben's fully naked well-muscled torso made me almost cream right then and there.

As Ben sat back up, he maneuvered himself to sit on the edge of the bed as I moved in front of him.

I tore my shirt up and over my head, flinging the material off to the side. But, before I could begin to unbuckle my belt, Ben shook his head, his hands reaching out to cover mine.

"No wait," he said, grasping my fingers to pull them away from my belt. "Let me do it." His words were breathless, but the eagerness on his face made me smirk.

"I'm not going to stop you," I said, as I raised both my hands to rest them behind my head.

Where Ben sat, he was almost at eye-level with my crotch, and I watched him neatly unbuckle and unzip my pants. He leaned forward, placing butterfly kisses on my bare stomach, as he tugged my pants down and past my hips.

The material dropped to the floor, and I neatly stepped out of them. And with only my briefs to hold it back, there was no disguising exactly how hard my cock was.

Glancing down, I could see how my dick stretched the material of my briefs. And Ben's face was now so close to it, a mere thrust of my hips would be enough to brush my shaft against his chin.

Ben ran his hand lightly across my briefs-covered shaft, his fingers curling around the thickness of my cock. "You're much bigger than I imagined," Ben chuckled, yet I heard the touch of apprehension in his voice.

Dropping one of my hands from my head, I reached down to cup Ben's chin, angling his eyes up to face me. "Are you sure?" I asked him, even as every fiber in my being was dying to slide my cock into his sweet tasting mouth. "We don't need to..."

Ben cut me off before I could finish the sentence. "I want this a lot." He paused for effect as he gave me a meaningful look. "Like, a *lot*. I've just never sucked a dick before."

Dropping my other hand from my head, I cupped his face in between my palms. "First time for everything," I said with a shrug and a chuckle of my own.

Ben's unsure look transformed into a grin as he chose that moment to begin to slowly stroke my shaft through my briefs. I could tell he knew exactly what his hand was doing to me, as I tried but failed to hold in a low groan.

That's when he finally took the next step and mercifully slipped my cock out of my underwear. I took in the eager glint in his eyes as my dick popped up right in front of his face.

His mouth was now so tantalizingly close to the glistening tip of my cock, as he curled his fingers around the base of my manhood. And his hot breath brushed against my shaft, sending heated shivers through my body.

I still held Ben's face in my hands, but I fought back the impulse to press my dick towards his lips. Instead, I let go of Ben's chin, dropping my hands to my sides.

"I need you to suck me off," I said, my voice tight and pleading.

Ben stared up at me, and we locked silent gazes. And, without another word, Ben opened his mouth wide and slipped my cock in between his lips.

I let out a small sigh of pleasure as his slick wet tongue slid its way all along my firm length. He kept pushing more and more of my dick agonizingly slowly into his mouth, but still my dick didn't quite get completely wet.

Ben made a small gagging sound, just before the base of my cock could reach his chin.

I knew my cock would be too big for him to swallow whole — *especially as this was his first time eating a dick* — I let Ben take the lead.

"Frumaph." Ben tried to speak around the part of my dick that was still in his mouth.

A moment later, Ben slid the rest of my dick out of his mouth before speaking again.

"Fuck," Ben said, more intelligibly this time. "OK, so I knew all about the gag reflex. But I *really* wasn't ready for it."

"You want to stop?" I asked, but Ben hurriedly shook his head.

"No, I don't want to stop. I'm just trying to figure out how to get it all in." Ben was now looking intently at my dick, as though he were trying to work out some kind of puzzle.

The intense look of concentration on his face was almost comical. And I bit back a small chuckle as I watched him figure out how to suck me off.

A few seconds later, Ben gave my cock an intense nod. "OK, I think I got it," he said, as he reached one hand around to cup my ass, the other still holding my shaft steady.

This time, Ben smoothly slid my dick into his mouth — right down to the hilt — until the tip of my cock met the back of his throat.

The friction of the roof of his mouth, as my cock head brushed against it, was incredible. It was enough to me rear back my head, and let loose a long low groan.

And I couldn't stop myself. I pulled my cock back, and Ben grasped my ass cheek holding me steady as I did. Yet before my cock popped out of his mouth, I thrust back in.

This time I couldn't keep my hands at my sides, I had to reach out and grasp his head to hold Ben steady as I slowly fucked his sweet mouth.

And Ben took every stroke in his stride.

"Yeah, like that," I groaned as I thrust into him again and again. "Suck it like that, just like that."

Angling my gaze down towards Ben, I watched as my firm manhood slicked its way in and out of his lips. "You like that don't you?" I grunted. "You like how it tastes..."

Ben hummed in agreement, and the thrum of his voice sent pleasurable tingles right down to my balls. It was enough to make me move my hips harder and with more urgency.

"Yeah, you do. God, you feel so good." I could feel heat begin to build. And the promise of an explosive orgasm began to dangle on the edge of my senses.

"Keep sucking it," I said with a grunting thrust so hard, my balls swung up and slapped Ben's chin. "It really feels so good..."

Ben moved his hand from my shaft and circled it around me to rest it on my ass. And his hands cupped my butt cheeks as I continued to thrust.

I was so close, so very close. But, I didn't want to cum in Ben's mouth.

I needed to cum. Yet I needed that release to be in a much deeper and darker part of Ben.

With all the willpower I could muster, I pulled my dick right out of Ben's mouth. Ben tried to follow after, his tongue poking out from between his lips, as he tried to shove my dick back in.

Reaching behind me, I grasped Ben's hands, gently tugging them away from my ass, as I took a step back.

This seemed to snap Ben out of his hungry search for my cock, and he gazed up at me curiously. "What's wrong...?"

I placed a finger on his lips, hushing him as I spoke. "I want to take you deeper."

Ben appeared confused for a second, before his features quickly transformed into a look of surprised realization. "Wait a second...you mean you want to...what, like... in the ass?"

I ran a hand through Ben's hair. "I'll make it feel so good. Promise. We'll go slow."

Ben gave me that same look of concentration — that he'd pointed at my dick earlier — as though he was trying to figure me out.

Yet it didn't take long for him to work out the answer to whatever question he had in mind.

"I've never put anything up my ass. That's not something I've ever thought about trying...you know?" I watched as Ben reached out to place a steady warm palm on my hip with a nod. "But let's do it."

Chapter 10

BEN

Shifting back further onto the bed, I tried to mask my nervousness as I busied myself with my belt buckle.

I'd imagined the possibility of anal, from the moment we'd entered Josh's room. But, the reality of the fantasy was more than a little nerve racking.

I had no idea what I was doing. All my life, my sex life had always been 100% straight-as-an-arrow. Until I met Josh.

I swallowed when I felt Josh's large hands gently reach out to cover my own. He now knelt up on the bed, his knees straddling either side of me.

"Let me." Josh's voice took on a calming tone, as he loosened my white-knuckled grip from my belt.

Slowly, he undid my belt and then my pants zipper. And I lifted my hips up into the air to allow him to tug the pants off my legs, until I was left wearing nothing but my loose boxers.

Tossing my pants off to the floor, Josh reach down an curled his hand around the tent that had formed at the front of my boxers.

I was rock hard and painfully horny. So I didn't bother hide my biting lip and long groan, as Josh gave my boxer-clad erection a couple of quick tugs.

I followed up that groan with a long sigh when Josh's hot lips began to kiss their way up my abdomen.

Soon enough, Josh was finally placing brief fluttering kisses on my lips. And each peck was punctuated by a whispered assurance.

"I'm...*kiss*...going...*kiss*... to make you feel...*kiss*...amazing." Josh said, as he reached past me towards the small bedside table next to the bed.

I angled my gaze over to see what he was doing, (even while I continued to return Josh's flurry of kisses), and noticed he'd grabbed a small bottle of something from the drawer.

Josh broke off his kissing flurry and indicated the small bottle with a wave. "I'm gonna need to lube you up," he said as he sat back on his heels, and rubbed his hand across my stomach.

His touch electrified me. And I was as curious as I was horny, about what was about to happen next.

Without another word, I flipped over onto my front. Josh was still straddling me, but he gave me enough room to swivel myself around in between his legs.

Face down, I could feel Josh now plant kisses on my back, in between my shoulder blades, making his way down my body to the crest of my ass.

He then made quick work of tugging my boxers down to my knees. And, soon after, I could feel Josh cup my butt cheeks.

"You're ass is so incredibly round and firm," Josh said from behind me.

I tried to peer over my shoulder at him, the awkward angle giving me just enough of a view to catch the tip of Josh's huge erect dick glistening with a bit of precum.

Glancing further up, I caught the mesmerized look on Josh's face as he continued to cup and pat my ass.

"Are you going to be doing that all night?" I said with a chuckle. "Or is there something more coming?"

Josh laughed as he tore his eyes away from my ass to meet my gaze. "Oh, something will definitely be coming tonight," he said as he twisted the bottle cap off the lube. "Now, simply relax," he continued as he parted my ass cheeks. "I need to lube you up."

I nodded, turning away to face ahead as I felt Josh's fingers smear some of the cool lube around my hole.

It felt nice. And I was wondering what all the fuss was about...right up until I felt the burn of Josh's finger begin to test my tight entrance.

I made a small sound of surprise, and I felt Josh's finger immediately stop moving. "Does that feel OK?" Josh asked me.

I glanced over my shoulder, giving him a confirming smile and a nod. "Caught me a little by surprise, is all. Keep going."

Josh nodded. "That was only one finger," he said as he returned to smearing up my hole with even more lube. "Tell me how it feels with two."

This time, I was ready for the burn of feeling Josh's two fingers pushing their way into my puckered ass. I released a breath I didn't realize I was holding when I felt him pull his fingers back out.

Yet I still felt I could take a little more.

"Good?" Josh asked me.

"More," was my single word reply. And I felt Josh already begin to prod at my entrance again with more lube.

Relaxing my hips, I readied myself for even more, preparing to have my tight ring stretched even further. And seconds later, I felt Josh slide in three lube-covered fingers into my ass, the digits entering me right up to the hilt.

So many fingers in my asshole had me grabbing the bedsheets to steady myself. But breathing through the burn, I focused on relaxing my anal muscles. And, after a few long moments, I started to feel my ass adjust to being so *stuffed*.

"And how does that feel?" Josh asked as I felt him curl one of his fingers inside me, using it to rub my inner walls.

It felt strange at first. And then Josh found a bundled knot of nerves inside there.

Once his fingertip brushed it, I felt an incredible heady wave of pleasure.

It was a powerful sensation, one that made my balls tighten as though I were about to cum right then and there!

I let loose a long slow groan that had Josh chuckling.

"So, I'm guessing that feels good then, right?" Josh asked as he continued to smooth his finger across my pleasurable spot.

I hummed in agreement, not trusting myself to say another word, as I reveled in the feel of Josh inside me.

And then he wasn't.

No sooner had I started to involuntarily grind myself against the bed in time with each rub of his finger, Josh pulled all three digits out of my ass.

"Wait, don't stop," I angled my gaze over my shoulder to see why Josh had stopped, but paused when I felt him part my butt cheeks.

I managed to get a look at Josh pointing his cock towards my ass. His face was a look of hungry concentration, as his hands spread my cheeks wider as he positioned himself.

As soon as I felt the very tip of Josh's dick brushing my tight entrance, he looked up and met my eyes with a grin.

And with that, he finally slid his long hard dick — inch by inch — into my ass.

Josh's three fingers had been enough of a stretch, but they didn't prepare me for how big his cock would be in their place.

I grimaced, pressing my face down into the bed, as Josh grunted his way carefully into my body.

It seemed to take forever. Yet, finally, after a few long seconds, Josh was laying flush against my back, balls deep in my ass.

His body pressed me down onto the bed, his muscled frame like a weighted blanket, as Josh stilled for a moment.

But then he was pulling back, slipping out of my asshole, his cock rubbing that pleasurable knot of nerves just right.

Before I knew what was happening, he pushed back into me again, firmer this time, and I grunted under the press of his hips.

"You are so tight," Josh's voice was low, his lips half-pressed against the back of my neck as he spoke. "I've wanted...*ugh*...you like this...*uh*...since I met you."

I moaned as Josh slowly fucked me, my hands returning to clasping the bedsheets tight, as I reveled in the feel of his muscled body pressing over and over into my own.

I could feel Josh thrust harder, his lips gone from the back of my neck, when he pushed himself up off my back. His arms placed either side of my shoulders, Josh was now able to pound himself into my ass.

The bed was rocking so hard, the squeaking was almost as loud as my groans and Josh's grunts. My cock was so painfully hard, that every thrust rubbed my dick against the firm mattress.

We both were moaning loudly, and Josh's voice sounded tighter, and I could tell he was about to blow. His long thrusts were now hurried pounds that had me on the very edge.

"I'm gonna cum," Josh grunted, never missing a stroke.

I closed my eyes, gasping with excitement as this man fucked me to the point of near-release. "I'm gonna cum..." Josh dipped his head and placed a kiss between my shoulder blades. "I'm almost there...Almost!"

It's at that moment that I decided to clench my asshole, making myself as tight as I could around Josh's cock.

And that did it.

"Fuck YES!" Josh yelled out, as with a final hard bed-shifting thrust, he exploded deep into me.

Chapter 11
JOSH

My eyes rolled back into my head once my orgasm hit.

Ben's slippery hole already had me on the cusp of one of the best orgasms in my life. Yet when his butt clenched around my manhood, I couldn't hold back.

Over and over, I pumped spurt after spurt of cum as hard as I could, before finally collapsing on Ben with an exhausted grunt.

I have no idea how long we lay there in silence — with me wordlessly gasping for air — while Ben soothingly rub the side of my hip.

Yet, once I found my voice, the only thing I could say was... *"Fuck."*

Ben laughed. "I was about to say the same thing myself," he said, as I began the long slow pull of my cock out of his hole.

I slumped over onto the bed beside him, as Ben turned over onto his side and faced me. "That was," I said with a shake of my head. I felt almost at a loss for words. "That was amazing."

Ben reached down a hand between us, his fingers curling around my softening cock.

I shivered slightly when his finger brushed my still-too-sensitive tip.

"I wasn't sure at first," Ben said, as his hand slipped from my dick to cup my balls. "But hell, that felt good. You weren't wrong."

"Yeah," I reached out, grasping the back of Ben's head to bring him into a quick hard kiss. "That was only the start."

Smoothing my hand down from the back of his head, I traced my fingers along his neck, until I came to rest my palm on his chest.

Lightly, I pressed Ben flat on his back, before moving to plant a kiss on his right pec.

I wasn't done with him yet.

I'd noticed that Ben's cock was still firm and very much ready for release. And I'd been dying to get a taste of his manhood from the moment I saw his profile picture.

Ben sighed as I kissed my way down his body, slowly making my way down past his navel.

Soon enough, I was hovering over Ben's cock, the sweet glistening tip of it inches from my hungry mouth.

Ben groaned, and I looked up at him, enjoying the frustrated almost pleading look in his eyes as I hovered there.

"Beg for it."

"Please," Ben grinned as he replied, reaching down to place a hand on the side of my face. "Please suck my dick off."

'Close enough,' I thought.

And, opening my mouth wide, I sucked in Ben's entire dick in one long swallow.

I slurped him into my mouth without hesitation, and went straight to work bobbing my head up and down on his cock.

I knew he was so close. I could feel the tension in his thighs as I clasped them, holding him steady as Ben humped up in time with my movements.

I could feel the veins of Ben's manhood with every slurp. And, no doubt, my earlier ass pounding must have brought him right to the teetering edge of orgasm.

And now I was going to do everything in my power to tip him right over the edge...*and down my throat.*

"Yes. That's what I need..." Ben whispered out the words as I tasted every inch of his length. I looked up at him, reveling in the sight of Ben staring down at me, his face a mask of ecstasy. And that is when I began to flick the tip of my tongue off the end of his dick with each long suck.

"*Oh!*" The sensation of my tongue flicking off his sensitive tip clearly took Ben by surprise, so with a hum and a grin, I did it again.

Ben bucked his hips up towards my mouth, his hands reaching out to grasp the back of my head as he steadied my face.

"That's it," Ben grunted as he bucked once again, the movement so hard and urgent, his balls slapped up and met my chin with each thrust. "Like that...ugh...suck it just...like...THAT!"

With a cry, Ben let loose into my mouth, the hot ejaculation spurting against the back of my throat. As I held Ben's hips in a vice-like grip, he pressed again and again into my mouth, and I swallowed every bit of his salty release.

Chapter 12
BEN

I don't know how long I lay splayed out on Josh's bed. All I know is that it took me a long time to catch my breath.

And with my eyes closed, my heart-raced as my body came down from the single best orgasm of my life!

I'd never had my dick sucked like that before. And I'd certainly never been taken in the ass like that before either.

And that was all I could even think about for long moments, as I enjoyed the butterfly kisses Josh placed across my abdomen — then up my chest — as he wordlessly worked his lips slowly up my body.

By the time my breathing finally slowed, Josh was laying flush over me. He was kissing me, his lips claiming my mouth with hard urgency, his tongue curling around my own.

I could taste cum in his mouth. And I grinned once I realized that Josh had swallowed my cum without hesitation.

Josh moved his lips from my mouth to place kisses along my jaw, before pausing to whisper in my ear. *"How did that feel?"*

I shivered at the heat of his breath against my earlobe. "You certainly delivered what you promised..." I said with a chuckle, watching as Josh reared his head back to regard me with a raised brow. "Earlier," I clarified, reaching up a hand to smooth away the curiosity lines creasing his brow. "You promised you'd make it feel good. And *boy* did you."

It took Josh a moment to register what I'd said, before he let loose a short bark of laughter. "I always aim to please."

Josh then gave me a long considering look, and I felt the easy post-sex intimacy between us suddenly feel a little tense.

I looked on confused as Josh sighed, hefting his weight off me and shifting to lay beside me. I matched his movements, rolling over onto my side to face him, not sure of what had suddenly changed in the last couple of seconds.

"Hey," I began as I reached out to trace Josh's jaw with my fingertips. "What's with the frown?"

Josh closed his eyes with yet another sigh, but I could feel him lean into my touch as he spoke. "I was just thinking about Arthur."

I grimaced. It was never a good sign when someone you've just slept with starts to bring up your parents. "OK, so this all just took a *really* weird turn..."

Josh scoffed as he rolled his eyes at me. "Not like that." He then ran a hand over his face, and I could almost feel his frustration in the action. "I was thinking about how on earth I'm going to face him next time I see him."

"Why? What's the problem?" I asked, only to have him roll his eyes at me again. "Seriously, you keep rolling your eyes at me, and I'll...well." I couldn't think of a threat scary enough to intimidate a man like Josh. I threw a hand up helplessly into the air. "Well...you think on that." I ended weakly.

Josh rubbed his brow, and my fingers itched to reach out and smooth away the frown on this face. "We have a code back at squad. Family's off-limits."

I couldn't hold back, I wanted to feel Josh again. Giving in, I placed a hand on his naked chest, rubbing his firm pecs.

Surprisingly, it seemed to do the trick.

Josh visibly relaxed, the tension from a moment earlier already beginning to ease. "I'm sure my dad will understand."

Josh gave me a skeptical look. "Understand that his former trainee rookie cop went and seduced his flesh and blood?"

This time it was my turn to roll my eyes at Josh. "First off, you didn't seduce me. Don't be so overly dramatic."

"Not all gay men are overly dramatic..." Josh sassed back, but I continued over him.

"Second of all, my dad doesn't have a problem with the fact that you're gay. So..." I shrugged.

"And he's fine with *you* being gay too?" Josh countered. And I fell silent.

It hadn't occurred to me till now, but everything I knew about myself sexually, had changed tonight.

When Josh and I had first stumbled into his room in a passionate haze, I was planning on simply writing this all off as a single night of experimentation.

But that was right up until it turned into a night of some of the best sex of my life. And all with an attractive man I felt comfortable with.

So, did this mean I was fully gay? Was I going to have to come out to everyone? Come out to my friends?...

"Come out to my dad?" I said aloud.

Josh startled me from my thoughts, when he replied to my question.

"Exactly." Josh punctuated the word with a short nod. "The old man may not be too pleased that I've bedded you."

I couldn't hold back a smirk. "Bedded? Dude, what century are you speaking from? I can't understand you with that thick Victorian accent. *And don't you dare...*"

I jutted a finger at Josh, catching him just as he was about to roll his eyes at me again. To his credit, he stopped himself mid-roll.

"Look, will you take this seriously for just one second, please." Josh said with an exasperated tone. "Arthur is one of my oldest friends. I really respect him. But this..." Josh indicated between us with a wave. "I'm not sure he is going to be fine with a cop doing his son. Doesn't matter if that cop is straight, gay, or anything in-between." Josh sighed, his eyes casting down and away from mine. "I think we shouldn't..."

Without hesitation, I clamped a hand over his mouth. Startled, Josh raised his gaze back up to meet mine with a puzzled look.

Not seeing Josh again, not being able to taste him or feel him pressed against me ever again, simply wasn't an option. And it took until this moment for me to come to that realization.

I wasn't sure where I was going with all of this, but I wanted to do this with Josh again. *And again and again.*

"Come to dinner with the family tomorrow." I said, and Josh's eyes widened.

He made to move his face away from my hand. Yet I continued to keep my hand clamped over his lips. "No, wait. Listen. My dad would be happy to have you round. And..." I rushed through the rest of my words when Josh started to muffle a reply through my fingers. "...it will be a chance for you to get over the hangup of facing my dad again. There," I said with finality, dropping my hand from Josh's mouth. "I'm done."

"You really want us to come out to Arthur as a couple?"

I shook my head hesitantly. I was no where near ready for that kind of step.

Besides, it has only been one night. A passionate mind-blowing night — but still just was one night. It was way too soon to know where Josh and I were going.

And even as that thought came to mind, I had to shove it away. I wanted more of this. More of laying down beside Josh as I smoothed away his frowns and worries.

It seemed like being with Josh had suddenly turn me into the sort of romantic my ex-girlfriends claimed I never was with them.

"No, nothing like that. Just dinner with the family. My dad was going to invite you anyway, he mentioned it to me yesterday."

Josh looked at me intently, as though he were trying to search for any trace of doubt in my mind.

This time, I was the one to roll my eyes at him. "Come on, it's not like you're asking him for my hand in marriage. It'll be like a regular dinner among friends."

Josh's features turned thoughtful as he regarded me a moment longer. "Just a dinner with friends," he began, before humming in agreement. "I think I can manage that."

"You'll see. You'll walk in there, and everything will be the same...only a little bit different." I said with a sense of confidence I didn't quite feel.

Josh finally cracked a smile, seeming to relax, as he reached up to clasp the hand I had resting on his chest.

"So..." Josh began, letting the word linger for a while before continuing. "Hand in marriage? The sex was that good, huh? Already thinking about me putting a ring on your finger..." Josh's smile widened as I sputtered a reply.

"Come on, I didn't mean it like that. It was a figure of speech. Dude..."

"Of course, of course. *Absolutely.*" Josh's tone and cocky smirk implied anything but agreement.

But before I could say another word, he leaned forward, and captured my mouth in a kiss.

THE END

Thank you so much for reading Hard Wright!

But wait! Don't go just yet! If you want to read even more steamy romance, check out my new series 'Love On Ryder Ranch'.

The first book in the 'Love On Ryder Ranch' series is available for purchase right now by visiting this link: https://books2read.com/u/38VewO

Or you can simply keep reading for a quick sneak peek into 'Hot Ryder'...

HOT Ryder

A Gay Cowboy Second Chance MM Romance (Love On Ryder Ranch Series)

By B.T. Haiyes

Chapter 1

AUSTIN

Five Years Ago

I felt my heartbeat pounding in my throat as I eased down on the brake, readying myself to make the hard turn around the corner.

My hands tightened, knuckles white, as I gripped the steering wheel, as I prepared to whip it round at the right moment.

If I wasn't careful, the car would get flung off the road... like someone riding a bronc without a saddle.

"Woah, Austin!" Brendan yelped, his hand braced against the passenger seat window as I whipped the wheel around.

My pickup truck responded exactly the way I knew it would, skidding hard around the corner off the main street into the side road.

"I'm not gonna slow down today! *Whoooo!*" I exclaimed as I sped down the empty road into the pitch black off-road ahead.

I knew all the streets of my hometown like the back of my hand. Having lived here all my life, 21 years is a long time to get to know a town like Katoka Hills.

This town was too small for me. Less than 4,000 folks lived here. Heck, my entire high school had fewer than a hundred kids in attendance.

I chuckled at the thought of my old school days, having barely graduated from that boring hellhole years ago.

I was an average student, getting by on C's and D's. And that would never be enough to get me a college scholarship — or give me a chance at a better life.

In the end, school taught me nothing that I could use in real life — other than how to stand up for myself in a fight, of course.

However, where I was going, I wouldn't need equations and books. All I needed was a ranch, a rodeo, and a roaring crowd.

I'd gotten all three — in spades — tonight. And now I had enough money in my pocket to make a real break for it.

That's because, just a few hours ago, I'd come first in our counties twice-yearly saddle bronc event.

I'd trained for it for months. And my best friend, Brendan, helped me every step of the way.

The rodeo show was a winner takes all event. The 'all' in question being a check for five thousand dollars!

And now me and my best friend were riding over to go hang out at the ridge and knock back a few beers in celebration.

It had been a hell of a day. I felt as though I was on the cusp of a brand new day, and well on my way to achieving my dream of becoming a saddle bronc champion.

I'd been working for this since I graduated.

I was never going to get into college, but I found work as a ranch hand on a couple of local farms. And, part time, I put in my dues as a Pickup Rider working at the Katoka Hills local rodeo, helping during rodeo season.

Now, at the age of only 21 years old, all of my hard work, blood, sweat, and tears, was paying off. *Big time.*

"Come on, slow the car down."

I looked over to find Brendan giving me a pleading look, his crystal green eyes wide. He and I were less than five months apart in age, yet he never quite had the sort of devil-may-care love for danger that I had.

"I know we're celebrating your win," Brendan continued through gritted teeth and a grimacing smile. "Let's at least try to make sure you're still alive to cash that winner's check later. OK?"

Rolling my eyes, I eased my foot off the accelerator, reducing our top speed from nearly 90 MPH down to what felt like a crawling 50 MPH.

"I don't know what you're worrying about." I angled my attention away from Brendan once I saw him relax into his seat with an exaggerated sigh of relief. "These roads are always empty." I lifted a hand off the steering wheel to wave at the desolate road ahead. "Especially at 2am in the morning."

"3:47am." Brendan quipped, jutting a finger at the clock on the dashboard. "Besides, Mr. Timm's farm is near here. Maybe he likes to take pre-dawn strolls along this roadside now and then. And so what then? You could have hit him."

"That's if he can even walk a straight line long enough to stay on the roadside." I bantered back, as I remembered how Mr. Timm was well known for spending late nights drinking away at the only bar in town.

He'd drunk enough — and slurred his way through enough bar fights — that Timm's almost had the reputation for being the town drunk.

Almost, but not quite. *That reputation was reserved for my dad.*

I grimaced, not wanting to think about my Old Man when I was supposed to be celebrating.

I glanced over at Brendan once, then twice, before giving him a cocky grin when he finally noticed me trying to get his attention.

"What?"

I put on my best country accent, thick and deep as I could get. "*You townie folk coming up here, telling us kind folk how to drive and whut to do...*"

Brendan chuckled as he joined in, matching me word for word as we both refrained Mr Timm's oft-repeated complaint, whenever he saw Brendan around town. "... *y'all should keep them city-slicking lifestyles to ya'selves.*"

We then looked at each other for a second, before bursting out into a round of belly-laughs.

"That guy is such an asshole," Brendan said as we guffawed.

Brendan hadn't lived in this town as long as I had. He'd arrived here as a teenager, less than six years ago, along with his mom and dad from the Big City.

Brendan told me that his parents wanted to move here so that the family could live a slower lifestyle. However, I don't think anything can actually prepare you for exactly how slow life in a town, like Katoka Hills, can be.

When Brendan first arrived in Katoka Hills with his family, he'd found himself instantly on the outs with some of the less-than-welcoming crowd about the town.

I did not care where Brendan came from. Besides, I was used to being an outcast myself, what with my family's rep and all.

So I didn't hesitate to dive into a fight, having Brendan's back against one idiot who'd jumped him.

And Brendan and I had been best friends ever since.

I never knew why he continued to hang out with me, even after graduation.

I was always getting into trouble when I was younger. While Brendan seemed to ace his classes and always tried to keep his head down.

Even now, Brendan worked part time at the town newspaper, while attending community college to work towards his degree. I, on the other hand, roughhoused it in the rodeo and on the farm.

We were as far apart in our everyday lifestyles as you could get.

Plus, Brendan's parents (unlike my parent), were the respectable type. His mom was a teacher, his dad was a veterinarian.

And in a town full of farmers, cattle herders — and rodeo maniacs — a veterinarian was as highly a respected job as you can get here in Katoka Hills.

On the other hand, I was the son of the town rapscallion. My mom had left him behind — to look after a three-year-old son alone — as soon as dad's career as a rodeo rider was over. *Gone in a single fall.*

My dad had been drinking away the memory of it ever since. And he hated how much I loved the rodeo.

"What you thinking about?" Brendan's voice brought me back from my reverie. I'd been silent a moment too long, and he'd noticed.

I shook my head. None of the past matters now. Only the future and good times lay ahead.

"Nothing." I shrugged off the concerned look in Brendan's eyes. Not wanting to bring down the mood, I quickly changed the subject. "Hey, we're almost there!"

Leaning forward, I could see the ridge of the infamous hill of Katoka Hills, right on the edge of town.

It was a spot that Brendan and I had found a few years ago. And it was the perfect place to knock back a few beers, as we'd talk about what we planned for our futures. It was also the best place I knew to watch a sunrise.

"Why here though?" Brendan asked, as I brought the car to a stop near the edge of the ridge and unlocked the car. "We could have gone and grabbed some drinks and food at Sally's all-night diner." Brandon said as he snatched the six pack from the back seat.

"Don't you remember?" I hustled around my truck and hopped on up onto the hood of the vehicle. "This spot is where I made all of those plans to become the Rodeo star I am today."

Brendan chuckled as he hustled onto the hood of the truck beside me. "Hey, don't get ahead of yourself," he began, as he pulled two of the beers from the pack. "The rodeo season has only started, and you need to keep practicing to stay sharp."

Brendan started to hand me one of the beers. Before I could clasp the bottle, he snatched it back, just out of reach. "Only the one beer. You are driving us back." Brendan said, as I leaned over and snatched the bottle out of his hand before he could move. "I'd rather we got back home in one piece — empty road or no empty road." Brendan continued with a small grin.

"Yes, *mom*." I groused as I popped off the bottle cap.

Brendan was always too careful when it came to living it up. He was always measured and practiced, and yet he'd rubbed off on me. I never would have had the discipline to train for the rodeo if he hadn't believed in me.

Plus, it was nice to know at least one person in the world cared if I lived or died.

"Fuck you, dude," Brendan laughed as he lightly punched my shoulder. "You know I'm only looking out for you," Brendan continued as he popped the cap off his beer.

"Yeah, I know." I took a long swig from my lukewarm beer, grimacing as the bitter liquid sank down my throat. I made a face as I turned the bottle in my hand, glancing at the label. "I should have cashed the check straight away. Bought us some real quality beers."

I glanced over to find Brendan making a similar face after he took a quick swig from his beer. "Sally's beers would have definitely been better." Brendan paused for a second, mulling that idea over. "Not by much. Still better all the same."

I don't know why, but looking at Brendan's unguarded profile — in the dim light of the burgeoning dawn — I felt a sense of camaraderie with him like I'd never felt before.

The hit of emotion surprised me. Maybe the excitement of the rodeo win — and a lack of sleep — were having an effect. Suddenly, I felt the need to pour out my heart a little.

"You were the only one who believed in me, you know that? Not even Mary-Anne did." I scoffed as I remembered my recent argument with my on-again, off-again ex girlfriend.

'Not such a loser now, am I, Mary-Ann?' I smirked at the memory, enjoying the vindicating feel of having proved her wrong. Hell, maybe she'd even come around again asking for me back.

Brendan glanced over at me, a look of confusion coloring his face. The puppy-like tilt of his head would have been comical if I wasn't feeling so damn emotional right now.

'Damn it, get it together', I groused at myself, quickly angling my eyes away from Brendan's curious gaze.

"Austin?" Brendan began as he patted my shoulder. "You OK there?"

I shrugged. I was never a 'talk through your feelings' kinda guy. I could make jokes or throw a punch. And yet, talking things out felt so much tougher.

"I'm going to leave town," I started, raising my eyes up to look at the sunrise. "That's as soon as I get a couple more wins, and save up enough money from my farm work." I eyed Brendan intently. "And I want you to come with me."

Brendan's eyebrows shot up in surprise. "For *real?*"

I nodded. "I know you have your job at the newspaper. And you're in the final year of college. A year will be plenty of time for me to get a few more wins under my belt." I nodded again, this time with confident finality. "After that, we can pack up and leave this town behind."

A wide smile, the widest I'd ever seen it, transformed Brendan's face. "I thought you wanted to stay in town a bit longer. Maybe get back together with Mary-Ann and move in with her."

I barked out a laugh. Mary-Ann and I only put up with each other out of boredom.

She and I kept getting back together because there wasn't much in the way of potential women in this town for me to hookup with.

Even Brendan was going through the longest dry dating patch I'd ever seen in a grown man. Likely because of the lack of twenty-something ladies in Katoka Hills.

Hell, I honestly can't remember the last time Brendan had gone on a date. And that's despite my trying to hook him up with a few ladies throughout the years.

I shook my head. "No way, that was never on the cards for me. The only person I'd stay in this town for is you." I gave Brendan a firm slap on the back. "If you come with me, we both can get out of here and get a place together in the Big City. Think of the major newspapers you could apply to. Especially once you get your qualifications."

Brendan simply stared at me, wordlessly giving me a long odd look, as though he were trying to figure something out.

"Well?" I asked finally, when the silence between us had drawn out long enough to feel a little awkward. "You wanna come with me or..."

"Of course I'll come with you." Brendan interrupted me mid-sentence, the odd look still on his face. I nodded at him with a grin and brought my beer bottle back up to my lips, thinking that was the end of that.

Yet Brendan continued speaking, the words hurriedly falling from his lips. "I love you, Austin."

I paused, the bottle halfway to my mouth, as I looked over at him. This was not something we'd ever said to each other.

Sure, if you forced to put it into words, I loved Brendan. The man was like family to me. Still, I was never into all of that flowery-talk stuff. My dad would have slapped the words from my mouth if I'd even said them to him.

I shifted uncomfortably with a quick sniff. "Um, sure," I began awkwardly, not knowing how to finish my sentence. So I settled for, "right back at ya.""

And then, before I knew what was happening, Brendan leaned over and planted a kiss on my lips!

To Be Continued...

To read the rest of 'Hot Ryder' you can find it right now by visiting here: https://books2read.com/u/38VewO

Want To Join My FREE Mailing List?

As someone who loves to read romance books, I always try to stay up-to-date with my favorite authors and their new releases. That's why I'd love for you to join my email list so we can keep in touch!

If you'd like to join, you can subscribe for free by visiting this link: bthaiyes.substack.com[1]

Sign up for my email newsletter, and you'll be the first to know about all my upcoming releases! As a subscriber, you'll also get exclusive offers and discounts on my books.

Plus, you'll even get a glimpse into my creative process with behind-the-scenes looks at how I write and develop my stories.

So sign up today to join a vibrant and expanding community of readers who have a passion for romance!

To subscribe, simply visit here: bthaiyes.substack.com[2]

1. https://bthaiyes.substack.com/

2. https://bthaiyes.substack.com/

ABOUT THE AUTHOR

Author B.T. Haiyes loves romance books, espresso and cheesecake — in no particular order.

Having started her freelance writing career back in 2015, she now carves out time in her work schedule, to write the kind of stories she loves to read.

Stories about men finding love in the most unlikely of places, are her particular favorites. Which is why she writes so much heartfelt MM insta-love short story fiction.

In her spare time — when she isn't writing or reading — she also likes to knit, cycle, and hike nearby trails.

Milton Keynes UK
Ingram Content Group UK Ltd.
UKHW010758110923
428455UK00015B/894

9 798223 183563